Dear Santa Claus

or How a Streetcar Came in a Stocking

written by Harriet Allen

illustrated by Patricia Eubank

Ideals Children's Books
Nashville, Tennessee
an imprint of Hambleton-Hill Publishing, Inc.

To Car
and Rosanna, William, Carlyle, and Winchester
With all my love.
—P.E.

Published by Ideals Children's Books
An imprint of Hambleton-Hill Publishing, Inc.
1501 County Hospital Road
Nashville, TN 37218

Library of Congress Cataloging-in-Publication Data

Allen, Harriet.
    Dear Santa Claus / by Harriet Allen ; illustrated by Patricia Eubank.– 1st ed.
        p. cm.
    Summary: A six-year-old boy asks Santa for one of the old streetcars being given away
by the Citizens' Street-Railroad Company.
    ISBN 1-57102-171-X (hardcover)
    [1. Santa Claus–Fiction. 2. Christmas–Fiction. 3. Cable cars (Streetcars)–Fiction.] I.
Eubank, Patti Reeder, ill. II. Title.

PZ7 .A42675 Dg 2000
[E]–dc21   00-059711

First Edition

The illustrations in this book were rendered in watercolor.
The text type is set in New Baskerville.

Cover and book design by John Laughlin.

David Douglas was seven years old. He could read and write as well as other boys. He could run as fast, jump as far, and spin tops with the best. As to play-fellows—nobody could excel his mother. David wanted to be a streetcar driver and his mother was his favorite passenger.

Then there was Jack, David's beloved dog. Jack was a short-haired yellow dog, always cheerful and fond of excitement.

One morning, about three weeks before Christmas, David was transfixed by hearing his father read an announcement from the morning paper that Mr. Miller's Street-Railroad Company was offering to give away old streetcars that would make good playhouses for children.

"Oh, papa," he cried, "could we get one?" His father made big eyes of astonishment at David, and pretended to be upset by the mere suggestion of such an idea.

"Mama, I know where we can put that car, if we should get it—
in our side yard! There's plenty of room."

"It would cost too much, dear."

"Mama," David said, brightening up, "didn't you hear? The
paper said they would give them away."

"So they will—but even a present is sometimes expensive. A
streetcar is so large, it would take horses and a big truck to move it,
and it would cost a great deal."

Very gently David's mother convinced him that it was out of the
question.

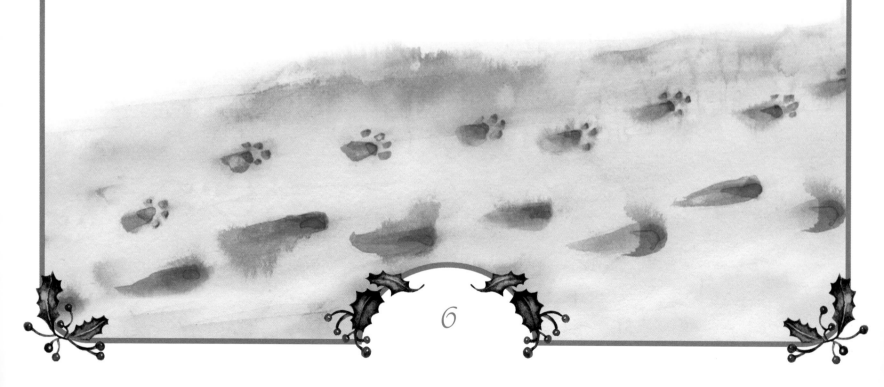

That night, as his mother tucked him into bed, David said, "Mama, why couldn't they bring the car on the track that runs in front of our house?"

"Because those cars have no wheels. It would just be a helpless old car all the rest of its life." She gave him a good-night kiss—and was gone.

Not far from David there lived a little boy whose name was Harold; he was not quite five years old. He lived in the same house with his grandparents and four aunts and three uncles—all of whom seemed to lie awake nights thinking what they could give him next. Harold liked having David come to play. David liked to ride the high-headed hobby-horse, and to work Harold's fire engine that squirted real water through a rubber hose.

One day, not long before Christmas, David went to play with Harold.

"I'm writin' to Santa Claus, David," Harold said. "I'm goin' to have him bring me a streetcar for Christmas! You can come and play in it, David; and I'll drive so fast you can hardly hold on!"

David's mind flew at once to the cars to be given away. Was Harold's car one of these? Hardly, he thought; Harold was asking Santa for his, and those cars belonged to Mr. Miller.

Suddenly, David realized that if Santa Claus was giving streetcars away, and you wrote the right kind of letter, then Santa would do the rest!

That night when his bed-time came, David handed his mother this letter to read:

Dear Santa Claus, Harold says you are going to bring him a Streetcar. Won't you please bring me one too. I am trying hard to be a good boy, and I want one very much.

—David Douglas.

His mother said, "I thought you had given up the idea of having a streetcar."

"Yes, mama, but this is different! If Santa brings it, it won't cost any money at all!"

"You know, David, if children ask for too much, Santa Claus might disappoint them. Will you promise not to be sad if it doesn't come?"

Oh, yes! He could promise that with a light heart.

David's hopes ran high. He sent Santa many letters:

Dear Santa Claus, Mama says a Streetcar is too much, but I do want it so much, and I'll be better than I ever was if you will please bring me one.

—David.

Dear Santa Claus, You needn't bring me a bob-sled if you will only give me a Car. I can use my old sled till next Christmas. *—David Douglas.*
P.S. I will do without the fireman's helmet too. *—D.D.*

Dear Santa Claus, Please bring me a Streetcar. If I had a Car I wouldn't need a hook and ladder wagon. Mama says I am a good boy.

—David Douglas

P.S. Even if it's a little broken it would do. I could mend it. I've got a hammer and some nails. Please leave it in our side yard. Goodbye.

—David Douglas

Dear Santa Claus,
    You needn't bring me
a Bob-sled if you will only
give me a Car. I can use
my old sled till next
Christmas.

        David Douglas

P.S. I will do without...

Christmas morning David woke early and ran to the window. He looked out upon a smooth surface of snow. There was no car! He crept back into bed, and shed a few unhappy tears. Soon however, he began to wonder what Santa had left in his stocking so he raced downstairs to see.

David got a fireman's helmet, new skates, and a lot of other treasures, and soon Christmas seemed pretty cheery.

19

Breakfast over, he and Jack set out to see what Harold had in his Christmas stocking. Just as they took the first turn in the drive, David's heart gave a great jump. He could see a great yellow and white streetcar in the midst of the snow. There was Harold, leaning out of the car shouting, "Hello, David! Hurry up! This car is ready to start. I told you Santa Claus was goin' to bring me this car. Get in!"

"Did you get a car?" Harold asked.

David's eyes filled and he shook his head. So Harold let David work the change-slide and the doors, and gave him all the coveted privileges. Then they went indoors to see the Christmas tree, and there was something there for David, too. He flushed with pleasure when Harold's grandpapa handed down books, candy, and a lantern, saying, "Santa left these things here for you David! They must have been hidden in his pack when he was at your house."

23

Later, as David started toward home, he was thinking that Santa Claus was very strange. His only wish had been a streetcar, whereas Harold had asked for that along with a lot of other pleasures. Yet Santa brought a car to Harold and not to David. He tried to think about his skates and fireman's helmet. After all, a streetcar was a tremendous gift to ask, even of Santa Claus.

He had almost reached home when he noticed that the fence was down and wagon wheels had cut the snow going through the opening into their yard. There stood a streetcar large as life; a beautiful yellow and white car with No. 11 in gold on the side. His mother was smiling, watching him. Then somebody said, "Well, sir, how do you like it?" and somebody swung David up to the front platform.

A big placard was hanging on the brake. David read the words: *"For David Douglas, from Santa Claus."* David laughed and kissed his mother and held his father's hand. He walked back and forth in the car. There was the cash-box and the brass slide for change in the front door. The brake worked and the bell-strap rang a real bell. Well, it was perfect!

FOR DAVID DOUGLAS

from

SANTA CLAUS.

"Wait!" said David's father. "I almost forgot the letter!" He began to read:

My Dear Douglas: I have taken the liberty of asking Santa Claus to deliver one of our old cars to your yard. Santa Claus showed me some letters from a young man by the name of David. I suddenly remembered what a world of fun there was in Christmas. I hope you will forgive me for getting my pleasure first and asking permission afterward. So please put this streetcar into David's stocking! I've never forgotten the time your mother made Christmas for me when I was a poor youngster with scarcely a stocking to hang. God bless you! You have a fine boy.

      Very truly yours,   *—John Miller.*

    P.S. This correspondence is a confidential matter between Santa Claus and me. No questions answered at this office.   *—J.M.*

David wondered why his mother, who had been reading the letter over his father's arm, turned suddenly, while she was smiling, and cried on his father's shoulder.